I0719320

Death and Afterlife on El Paseo
Cover art by Douglas C. Granum.
Cover design by Scott Norris

douglasgranum.com | monkeyhouse-media.com
ISBN 978-1-939723-24-6

First Edition

DEATH & AFTERLIFE ON EL PASEO

"When you love, you
complete a circle.
When you die, the circle
remains."

Once in what now is a faraway distant land there was a little West Highland white terrier who lived, in joy and happiness, with his lovely white-haired old mistress, Mary, in splendor and peace in their gentle oasis in Palm Desert, California. I'm that little white terrier, even though I am not short—I am tall for my breed.

My velvet, heedless days were filled with hot southern sun, warm love, and attention to my every need. You don't really know what hot is until you live in the desert. In the desert, where the air is bone-dry, there are cacti, roadrunners, palm trees, swimming pools, golf courses, hot asphalt, orange trees in blossom, dates and so much more. In the desert, the mountains are distant, edged with purple, and everywhere you look are flowers. I love the desert. In the desert, when it is 100 degrees, everything is 100 degrees: the rocks, the roads, the houses, the heated sky. The air in the desert is redolent of peace and quiet, of soft beauty.

Mary's house had a pool with blue tiles and tiles of mermaids on the bottom. An atrium…a large bronze sculpture of a seated Navajo woman by Allen Houser… a white Yamaha grand piano…lime green sofas, purple chairs with human feet in chrome, chairs at the bar made out of clear plastic that swiveled. A stainless steel fireplace. A dining table made of one grand chunk of jet ebony. A sunken bar with a sink. There were modern paintings on the walls, large photographs of horses, and doors, and windows of glass.

You see—to carry her story forward—she was wealthy. She had homes in California, a mansion on Puget Sound in the Pacific Northwest, and a grand chalet overlooking the Boulder Mountains 6,500 feet up in Sun Valley, Idaho.

You will probably hear this again, but she fed me rotisserie Greek lemon chicken hot off of the grill. What is it about lemons?

Once after a party, I ate a whole candy dish full of hard supper sweet tart lemon drops. They were beyond belief good, but, oh, did my right abdomen kill me. Mary called Saul, who came with his white-and-gold sports convertible. They took me to the vet emergency, where they pumped my stomach. I lost my taste for lemon after that, but Greek lemon chicken? Well, that's quite different.

As my precious Mary cared for me, I

supported her. We leaned into each other for most everything we did. She was calm and kind with me, and I was naturally sweet and gentle with her. Whenever she did almost anything, even the hot tub, she wanted me to be and I wanted to be by her side.

When we sat together on our lime green sofa in the grand expanse of our living room, watching John Wayne movies, we leaned against each other. She explained the plots to me, and I looked at her just like I could understand her. She wouldn't try to talk to me if I were sleeping.

When we were in the Mercedes, with our sweet maid Angela driving, I sat on Mary's lap with my head out the window. I knew which button to push to make the window go down. Every now and again, she reached into the pocket of her white cashmere sweater and pulled out some Bon Bon, and while holding it like a piece of fine gold in the palm of her soft upturned hand,

I would look at her sweetly, and she would chuckle softly and say, "For you, Josh." I would then gently lift the morsel off of her palm, pop it into my mouth, and while chewing, watch the Bentleys and Rolls Royces whisper past.

You can see she was kind. I was fed rotisserie chicken for dinner. My favorite was—well, I already told you, Greek lemon chicken hot off the grill from the deli section in Jensen's grocery, where we often went to shop.

At Jensen's, I rode in the grocery cart while Mary walked along, idly buying whatever caught her fancy. Sometimes she would buy three jars of peanut butter or large packs of paper towels that threatened to displace me in the cart. Once in a while, Jensen's would be offering little sautéed frankfurters. Mary always took a toothpick and plucked one off the plate and then broke it into chunks for me to eat. She wiped my mouth with napkins that Jensen's provided.

Even now, as I lie here in front of the fireplace looking into the flames, I can still see her standing in her spacious tile-lined kitchen. Frank Sinatra on the radio, desert sun slanting in over the San Gabriel Mountains and across her delicate frail shoulders, pulling off little morsels of hot moist white meat, I liked the white better than the dark, pulling those little nuggets of white succulent bits of chicken off the steaming carcass and popping them into my white mustached mouth. The juice ran down my cheeks, and she, as always, was ever-ready with a tissue to clean me up. She was always so good to me because she loved me. She loved me like a terrier loves—without reserve. She always talked sweetly to me, and I was forever in love with her because she loved me in return. True love is like that. She use to say that I had all the bad habits a good dog should have. between you and me, I don't think I have many bad habits.

Sometimes when she was drinking Absolut, her favorite vodka, she would hold me close to her face, tears in her eyes, and call me dolce. At times when she was drinking, we would talk a lot about George, her husband, who disappeared in a ceremony.

You can see here, I just wasn't like most other dogs you see or read about, the ones that tear up the couch pillows or scratch doors when they want in. When I wanted to get in, I just jumped straight up and down in from of the glass door, not touching it, until she saw me leaping up and down. She always laughed when she let me in. When she let me in, she would say "Oh, Josh," and touch me on top of my silky white head while tussling my hair. I loved it. I lived for it.

To love someone and want to be near them isn't something you can explain but rather something that radiates through your whole body.

Love has vitality, love is long lasting and solid and yet…and yet, it is fleeting.

Maybe my story is your story. This is my story; someday, tell me yours.

Mary was very different from anyone else I ever saw while we were together.

Mary had two daughters—neither like her but both kind. They had their own problems, but what do I know? They lived in a different place, so I never saw them much.

Mary drove a white Mercedes with soft tops and ivory leather interiors and chrome shiny wire wheels. She loved white, and so we always matched. Even if she wore mint green or sky blue we still matched. Ehat doesn't go with white?

She wore big rings, had short white silky hair like mine, and a dazzling smile. Her smile was her trademark. She was quiet, but when she smiled, my sun came out, and even though she didn't say a word, it was as if she spoke volumes. She always wore outsized huge rings. She had neckties made out of diamonds, tiaras that were like fireworks on top of her head, bracelets of silver and gold, crystal wristwatches with no hands. She was modern, and everyone remarked on her, her glasses and me. We were a couple, and it showed.

Did I tell you I am what you humans call a West Highland terrier? Though among we terriers, we are known to each other as bringers of doom to rodents.

I am white, silky smooth, fourteen inches tall, and when Mary and I went any-where, she put her braided white leather leash on my white rhinestone collar. Well, I can tell you without reservation that we looked pretty good walking down El Paseo. Yhat's the elegant shopping street in Palm Desert.

When the temperature was over 100 de-grees, which my Mary loved, the sidewalk set my feet on fire. I ran from shady spot to shady spot as much as I could, what with being on a leash.

On this street, there is much to see and a lot to smell. There are all sorts of dogs on this street. Little terriers the size of pigeons, Afghans sleek and dangerous, poodles of all kinds, and the occasional bird on someone's shoulder all wandered the heated streets with their elegant owners.

On El Paseo, Mary shopped almost daily, shuffling along, peering into the gloriously decorated windows. There were satin dresses, gems and jewels, perfumes and chocolates, cigars and art. When in Saks, I lay quietly under the skirt rack or near her while she endlessly tried on shoes, though there is no room in her closet for more shoes.

Funny about ownership. We dogs live pretty frugally, if you think about it. But I suppose buying too many shoes is like the burial of a bone. Something feels right and good when I bury a bone. I could see the same look on Mary's face when she bought shoes.

The sales people knew us by name and had little crunchy dog bones for me and water in a crystal Lalique bowl with an ice cube. We hung out at Gucci and the candy store across from the Beaux-Artsrestaurant.

In those days, I had my bath at Pampered Pouches every Friday morning with Jason. I liked Jason. He had tattoos, long hair like mine, only purple, and chains of gold around his neck. Like clockwork, I had to be ready for the inevitable parties we had every Saturday night. Saturday parties were stand-up affairs, and the people at these soirées, as Mary called them, wore some pretty nice shoes.

I had my teeth polished once a month as well as my nails trimmed. I slept in our king-sized bed with its pink-teal silk duvet cover and with my head on her pink silk pillow right next to Mary. She liked this since sometime before I came to live with her, her dearest George had died, and she said she liked to have me close to her at night. She was lonely.

I didn't know anything about loneliness then. I had never been lonely since I came to Mary as a pup.

Well, as you can imagine, I loved her with all the love a terrier can have, which if you know anything about terriers then you know that's a lot of love. We were quite the unique and handsome pair. When we were walking down the sidewalk, people called me by every name except Josh. They called me sweetie pie, poochie, whitey, darling. All this was okay—they didn't know better. They didn't know that I came from a long noble family from the Isle of Skye in Northern Scotland. We always attracted attention because of her, because of me. We, indeed, were quite the pair.

When we went to the Beaux-Arts for lunch or the Les Vallières—very French and very fancy—for dinner, I always slept with my head on her foot under the table. The world looks different when you see it from under a table, not to mention if you are not so tall. At Les Vallières we ate out of doors in the garden court under the spreading eucalyptus trees. Every now and then, Mary would quietly slide her hand under the table and slip me some morsel of calves' liver or sweet breads or a meaningless nothing of French bread sopped in boeuf bourguignon sauce.

Delightfully, during the dessert course there could be a dab of whipped cream off the top of some crème de la crème served off her white nail-polished finger and into my mouth. When Mary (or anyone for that matter) gives me a treat, I don't snap and grab like some ill-bred mutts; rather, I gently take it into my mouth. Finally, after these meals, she would invariably carry home some veal chop or other treat in some of the fanciest doggie bags you have ever seen for me to dine on later.

Driving home through the 90 degree warm desert nights, my head out the window smelling the palms, plumeria blossoms, freshly cut golf course grass, dry desert air, the night alive with a thousand scents, life was a ball. Speaking of which, I do love to chase balls, but I digress, for how could have guessed that all this would ever change?

I remember the stars in the desert so clearly, and some nights when I felt the voices of my ancestors calling to me across the ages, I would go out on hole eleven. That's where our home was. I would sit out there up on the tee box in the cool night grass by myself, looking up at those reefs of clear twinkling stars and that watermelon moon, and I would howl. It would just come over me: this sense of loss that I didn't (at that time) know anything about. How could I know anything about loss when all was bliss?

We liked to bathe in the morning sun before the day got too hot. Sometimes I would plop myself into the blue-and-gold hot tub with the mermaids on the bottom and take a few laps. I would then crawl out and shake a few times before crawling under Mary, asleep in her chaise lounge with her green cowboy hat over her face.

In a sort of sweet trance, I would finally fall into a peaceful sleep. You see, I was always next to her.

Late one morning the phone rang in the house, and I raised my head from my slumbers to see our maid coming out the French double doors with the phone in her hand calling, "Mary? Phone!"

As my Mary took her lime-green cowboy hat off her face, she turned round on the chaise, standing to take the phone. She breathed in like she was going to call me. Then she looked quizzically at me and then fell onto the grass, her head just a foot or so away from mine where I lay beneath the lounge.

She opened her eyes, looked at me warmly, and said "Oh, Josh" like she was surprised, and she closed her eyes again, and then the maid ran yelling through the lush flower garden to the neighbors. Our neighbor lady came running with a blanket and a pillow. They stood talking for a few minutes until a truck came with the screeching siren sound that I had heard often in that town of older people.

Someone from the truck, someone I didn't know, roughly and unceremoniously put me in the house. I ran to the low window in the dining room, watching as they put my Mary on a cart, then put her into the back of the truck with its flashing lights, and   finally drove quietly away. It siren didn't sound.

When you lose someone, your entire history together goes with them. When Mary disappeared into the truck with the flashing lights, she never came back. Then, when she never came back, all of our history together went with her. We own our history, but we don't own someone else's.

Our mornings in the sun. Our walks on the streets lined with date palms, flowering ocotillo, nopal cactus, and purple and pink bougainvillea. On our morning walks, she never had me on a leash, so I was free to run to both sides of the quiet elegant streets. I ran heedlessly this way and that under fragrant grapefruit trees with their yellow pendulant fruits, never knowing there was a new world far to the north. There were cold, invigorating, dripping, somber cedars where one night I would be involved in a fight for my life with a demonic black raccoon, hissing and slashing.

As I happily ran from one side of the street to the other, I often came to large fences surrounding palatial Spanish mansions. On the other side of these wrought iron fences were growling, spitting, barking Doberman Pinscher guard dogs.

As I put my little black nose against the cracks in these walls and fences, I caught glimpses of deeply troubling black vicious eyes that said, If there were not a fence, you would die a short quick, painful death. But then, I was not to be a red-and-white rag in their mouths—for they were fenced, and I was not. As I ran down the street from side to side, I barked and pranced, and I was happy they were not and never would be like me. This was another thing I loved about dear Mary: she was free and so, also, was I. I can tell if a dog is free or if it is a slave—there is something apparent about a slave dog or a slave person. They coil into themselves.

They don't look at you. They hold their tails down. Their fur lacks luster and body. Their eyes are sad and hostile, and their walk declares, I have lost and I don't care and have given up. Look at me and see how angry I am, they say.

I never rage at these poor penned creatures. I never rage at all; raging at life is tiresome, raging is for ill-bred garbage-can types, raging is coarse. Raging rarely gets results. I won't allow myself to rage. I prefer to discover, to look forward. There are always new dogs, new humans, new streets, new roads, new sounds, new nights, new days. Rage if you must in your loss, but rage instead against your own anger. Dogs and humans that are chained rage, for that is all they know, often chaining themselves.

I didn't know why then (but I know now), but I went and jumped up on our bed and howled until I fell into a scary sleep. Nobody came back that night, and the next morning when the door opened, it was her daughter. She picked me up and said, "She's gone, Josh." Then she put her face in the silky white fur at my neck and started to cry. Her face was grief-stricken and horribly distorted.

She carried me through the house crying, out into the yard crying, and finally sat down in the outdoor atrium crying, where she whispered, Oh, Mother. When she looked at me, I lay my ears back softly, looking deeply into her eyes. What I saw there made me afraid. Her eyes were rimmed with red, and tears were flowing freely down her cheeks. Her breath was sad; her mouth was twisted. I began to howl while her tears fell on my head. What had happened? My stomach hurt.

On the second morning after my dear Mary went away, the second daughter arrived. Coming quietly into our bedroom, she gently lifted me off of our bed where I was sleeping warmly, and she set me on the floor.

No "good morning, Joshie," no sitting down beside me on the bed as I woke up. What happened next was the beginning of a series of rude and rotten mysteries. The maids, the sisters came into our bedroom and began to take all of Mary's clothes, sheets, shoes, dresses, purses. They took everything and put it all in boxes. Then two big guys who made me growl, even though I don't usually growl, came into the house. They touched and packed Mary's remaining things in boxes. You're damn right I'm going to growl over something like that.

Something to understand here. Mary was a sumptuous dresser. Her clothes were representative of a lifetime's talent at picking remarkable, original works of wearable art. She was an early architect, and it was all design for her. Short-waisted bolero jackets of turquoise calf's leather, flowing silk

Indian knee-length curry-colored summer coats, white glossy leather pants, red socks, Italian lime-green loafers, cowboy boots. I was there when she shopped.

Diamond tiaras, rings with important stones from important collections. Leather chokers with ruby studs. So many beautiful objects, but then beautiful objects have no protection. No more so than her collection. Swaths of her life's choices of fascinating objects went to the Cathedral City Goodwill in Coachella Valley.

Her Frank Sinatra collection of 78s, "My Way." Gone. Her Tony Bennett charcoal sketch, "I Left My Heart in San Francisco" signed by Bennet. Gone. Cut glass stemware for seatings of twenty-five. Plates from Severus. Gone to Cathedral City. Our purple sheets and matching silk duvet covers and pillowslips. Gone. Towels, placemats, small hand-blown glassware. A house full of her books and drawings. Gone.

Cuisinart pots and pans. Gone. Even my sterling silver water food dishes, history, my history. I travel alone. No fences, endless eternity. Where am I going?

Yesterday's breakfast that we shared by the pool in the warm early morning sun, now in the garbage, I could still smell the bacon.

The big guys took away all the boxes of Mary's things, and that was that. I couldn't even find a sock or a shoe to remember the sweet scent of my mistress. All of it was taken. You understand that I am a Highland terrier—our sense of smell is what attracts us to each other. My sense of smell is some 100 percent greater than your human sense of smell. I could tell where Mary was in the house just by sniffing the air for her sweet flowery scent. When everything of hers was taken away, it was as though someone had burned all of her photographs. My joy was her scent, and now nothing. As I searched the house for something of hers, the door slammed, and I was by myself again. One of the sisters had put some dry dog food she'd bought at the store in a red plastic picnic plate. I have never tried dry dog food. Mary was never satisfied with the store-bought dog food, so she made her own.

The sister left some water in a kettle, which had some sort of colorful beetle floating in it.

I was now looking at a very tall closed purple door. A silent, dark house with the sweaty smells of the big movers still ruining the air. The sisters had left. A crumpled shirt from one of the movers lay on the floor. There were several bouquets of flowers that had arrived. These flowers were on the floor by the front door.

What to do?

I did what I always do when I feel like that: I went into our bedroom, jumped up on the bare mattress, and sniffed to see if

I could bring back Mary—there was just the faintest fragrance of her. I sat down and howled. My heart was broken, and I didn't know what was going to happen to me next.

It is easy to be a genius when things are going your way, but when things aren't, that's where the real genius sets in or falls away. I heard the Chihuahua next door barking excitedly as his master came home, and I felt fear and longing in the pit of my stomach. Fear because I didn't know what was going to happen to me; longing because I so missed Mary, whom I had almost never been away from. I looked with sad eyes at the darkening empty room, curled myself up in the tightest ball I could, folded my white fluffy tail over my eyes, and passed my second night alone. Even though it was warm, I felt cold.

The next morning, I had some leftover scrambled eggs from the girls' breakfast since I had not eaten any of the dry food and wasn't about to—and the girls knew it.

Next, they filled Mary's car with all sorts of stuff, and the tall blonde sister made a little bed for me in the front seat. I didn't want to sit in the front seat, so I jumped out of the car, but I was scooped up and put back in the front seat again. I jumped over the seat into the pile of stuff in the backseat and sat glaring at the sister as she got into the driver's seat and slowly pulled around and out the driveway. I wedged my way up to back window of the car and looked without believing or understanding as we drove out of that driveway. Do you ever just feel like moaning and bawling? That's what I did. I cried, cried, cried until the blonde told me to be quiet. And when I still cried, she tried to hit me with a map. "Won't you just stop crying?" she said with tears in her eyes. So I did.

Gradually, I closed my eyes and eventually fell asleep. I was drifting and dreaming as the blonde sister took us though Joshua National Forest. The morning and the anguish of leaving sank me into a deep sleep. I dreamed of one Christmas when we went shopping at Denise Robergé on El Paseo with the happy young blonde girl whom Mary introduced to me as her granddaughter. Mary and her granddaughter always laughed and giggled a lot when they were in fancy rock and old shop. Mary tried on great stone rings of all colors. They put collars of bright rocks and rings and things around their necks.

I briefly awoke from my dream as a large truck roared by and then just as quickly tumbled back into my dreams.

I saw the granddaughter, chrome blonde, reach down and pick me up. When the granddaughter took me shopping, we always went where there were young girls and strong flowery smells that hurt my nose. Sometimes it would take a day to get my scent back. Sometimes when we walked down the street she would rather unceremoniously pick me up and carry me down the street, laughing at everything and everybody. One afternoon, I remember the granddaughter stopping outside the open air sidewalk windows of the Beaux Arts restaurant. While we stood there, a nice older lady sitting at a table reached out and gave me in a French fry with ketchup. A first for me. And good. The granddaughter held me and wiped my mouth with her sweet perfumed handkerchief then.

The air was so warm and perfumed. I could smell all of the dishes they cook at Beaux Arts as the staff walked by with their trays of foods. The granddaughter held me tightly and just at that moment, as I was smelling her dream perfume, I felt the car slow down and woke, still smelling the warm asphalt smell of El Paseo and the sweet perfume on the granddaughter's handkerchief. The car turned sharply, rumbled for a time, then stopped. The blonde rolled up her window and shut down the engine.

Everything was quiet. The radio went off and instead of music I could hear rain pelting the roof of the car, and then I heard the blonde exhaling a loud sigh, saying, Josh I'm exhausted. You stay. I'll be right back. She opened the car door and got out and then shut the door, leaving me alone in the car. I heard all of the locks in the car click to keep me in.

As I sat up, I saw we were in a village at night but not like Palm Desert. The lights were high golden stars, like lamps with rain falling through them. As I watched, the blonde walked away through the insistent rain. Passing her was a person who turned around and looked after her when she had passed. He was dressed in a shiny tan plastic-looking long coat with a broad brimmed slouchy hat. He was carrying a bag. He put his face right up to our window. I growled very furiously, and then I barked, biting at the window, our faces only separated by the glass. The person quickly pulled back and hurriedly slouched away. I finally curled up on the blonde's warm seat to wait for a long time, the rain ceaselessly falling.

I was listening for the door latches to open the door.

From the same door where the blond had gone in, she finally came out. Unlocking the car, she opened the rear door. A cold wind and mist blew in and around me. She took out a box and my bowl, closing the car door with her foot. She opened mine and told me to jump out, forgetting to put my leash on me.

What is it that goes through most dogs' brains when they feel freedom? No fence, no traveler clothesline, no vibrating teeth chattering from electric fencing jolts, no leash, no rope. Freedom is something that I have had copious amounts of over time, yet it is always that moment when you can run-run-run like the summer wind that comes to me anyway. That most dogs just take off, down the beach, up the road, through the neighborhood, or just roll madly remains a mystery to me.

I jumped out of the car right into a puddle of cold rainwater. It was foggy and misty, just as had welcomed itself into the car. I walked under the car and took a long drink of fresh, delightfully cool rainwater from a small pool there. The blonde called me again and again, "Josh, come here right now," But I didn't. There are only two people in my world whom I come to: one is Mary, and the other is the artist who comes with the blonde and their two blonde children when we bring the Christmas tree into the house. Josh, she called again, and then, Josh, get over here now. I didn't and then walked out from under our car to the car next to it and then under another. Then under several otherd until I came to a tree with a little patch of grass that had been much marked by hordes of other dogs. I walked around and sniffed here and there while the rain pelted me. Finally, I found a slender green young alder. I sidled up and lifted my leg and left my contribution, like a Jackson Pollock painting with and on top of all of the other contributions on that side of the tree. Only difference here was you used your nose to read this tree, not your eyes.

As I stood there doing it, the blonde quietly, stealthily, crept up behind me and put my leash over my head. Good for her, I suppose.

I slept most of the night on a towel locked in a small bathroom with a single lightbulb. Something dripped constantly. The door was tall and narrow with a map on it of what to do in case of a fire. The toilet ran and kept me awake, in case the dripping weren't enough. The room was cold; it smelled like disinfectant, the kind that the pool man used each week in Palm Desert. There was water in my glass bowl from the desert with a few hairs and a dead bug floating feet up in it. Nearby was a plastic doggie box, something uneatable, it turned out. I thought of Mary. I scratched at the door. Nothing. I sniffed under the crack in the door and smelled everything from people's feet that I didn't recognize, toothpaste, and somewhere the smell of another anxious dog. Sniffing deeply I found the smell of someone smoking and the smell of someone crying. It has a smell all its own. It just came over me again how unhappy I was that I started to howl and then, for whatever reason, I started to bark, low at first and then louder. I became constant, the way I used to do it when I had our neighbors' white long-haired cat trapped in the lemon tree in Palm Desert. The blonde, with her pajamas on, jerked open the door so fast that I was still howling in her face. She reached down in the darkened bedroom and said, Don't you ever breath? How can you bark so much? and then she smiled at me and, laughing, picked me up shut off the little bathroom light and carried me to her soft and cozy bed. Oh Josh, you miss her, too, don't you? She start to cry before rolling over onto her side and pulling her knees up and then pulling me into the curve of her body next to her.

As I lay there, wrapped in her warm encircling arms, I could feel her sobbing while I watched the little red light blinking—red, green, red—from the lifeless television screen.

After a long time she stopped crying and finally went to sleep. I could smell her breath, which smelled sad and injured.

I jumped down from the bed, went to

the sliding door, and looked out from behind warm thin brown plastic curtains. Raindrops were running down the window and making everything blurry. Wind gusts picked up small bits of paper, an empty plastic bottle, and it turned a person's umbrella inside out.

The night was wet and stormy with large lakes of mud puddles and interlocking rings of raindrops. The whole scene was lit by yellow metal halide lamps. Everything glisten yellow and silver. The old café, closed right now, looked tired. The truck tire repair shop looked dark and oily. A large truck driving fast went by, and I suddenly felt very tired as well. I went back into the sad dark room, jumped up onto the bed, snuggled up next to the blonde, turned around three or four times, scratched a little nest on top of the bedspread, and curled into a tight ball.

The blonde put a warm arm around

me, muttered something in her sleep while I slipped off to dream as well, listening to the vanishing sounds of rain flowing from a dark distant roof.

Then nothing.

Chapter 2

We drove alvl the next day and all that day I fitfully slept. I woke myself up several times, kicking my legs while making strange little yelping barking sounds.

The blond rigidly focused white knuckled on the wet slippery highway,

told me to shut up.

Now and again, I raised my head to look around. There were no more palm trees. I particularly love Palm trees since one of the first things I did each morning was to rub my sides and back on the old hairy giant Palm outside of Mary's front patio. The warm sun, the warm sun of the south, the warm sun of the desert, all of which I love, was now deep roiling gray and every so often even heavier rain blasted the windows while the wind gusts rocked the car from side to side.

Cars, hissing blobs, were everywhere. There were misty distant mountains and partially flooded valleys, inundating rain-soaked farms. Everything was wet and weeping. Racing across rusty green bridges I caught glimpses of brown muddy roiling rivers.

The whole miserable scene took on a black and white photographic look, the color was washed out and gone.

I am hungry and thirsty something I had never been with Mary. When I lived with my Mary, I ate when I was hungry, drank when I was thirsty, slept when I became sleepy.

The most hurtful thing about sorrow is the way it invites the crowding in of memories of happier times for poignant comparison with one's present misery, and I was miserable.

Drifting around in the car from time to time I would catch Mary's scent from some object of hers that had been jammed into the car.

Sometimes I whimpered and even though the blond treated me well enough, she still would yell loudly at me to shut up, shut up, SHUT UP.

I knew she was suffering her loss as well, after all it was her mother who she lost.

Even so that is something Mary never did; she never raised her voice.

Can't a guy miss someone without being yelled at?

Humans forget that we of the dog family have very acute and a-tuned ears and accurate hearing, a whisper works as well or better than a shout.

Humans forget a lot of things about us dogs, in fact most people know very little about how we dogs think, how we hear, how we scent the world around us. How, if we are mistreated, how we can hate.

Conversely, how thoroughly, deeply we can reciprocate with love when shown love. Plus, on a deeper and instinctual level, it is we dogs desire and joy to protect those we love.

We are not little people though sometimes Mary called me her little man. But you see we canines come from a long and equally distinguished family as humans. It is not an exaggeration to say that without us dogs, you humans would never have gotten so far so fast in this world.

We terriers love people however we are

not people, even though now I admit I was treated like one.

The relationship between us dogs and you humans is a bond going back to the beginning of time, some two million years.

We have learned a thing or two from you, perhaps you have learned devotion from us?

I know this, there is a type of love that gives everything yet asks nothing.

My great great-great-granddaddy Angus was of this type. Fighting the encroaching English was his highly respected ability. Angus could scent the acrid smell of an English man a mile off.

When his old master, Peter Stewart, owner of the now famous, Elandonan castle died Angus followed the funeral processions to the church where Peter Stewart, was buried in a carved, sculptured niche in a stone wall of stacked and cemented shale. When the wailing bag pipers finally played

"Over the sea to Skye", every one left, Angus stayed. He was finally scooped up and taken back to the island castle of Elandonan, his home, where he immediately struck out that night in heavy winds and pelting rains from Loch Long.

Bedraggled and exhausted he gained the deserted church graveyard once more, wet and muddied. He scented out the niche where Angus Charles Stewart was interred. He stayed, howling and moaning, until he died three weeks later of starvation, he refused to eat.

The legend on the whole of The Isle of Skye, was that he died of a broken heart.

We highland terriers are known for our strength but then no one can live forever with a broken heart.

We Scotties are doers this world and like to participate. We may not be able to speak the human language, but we have a vast language of our own that you humans can only guess at. There are some good things about not understanding the language of those around you as well as some bad but not all bad.

All around we dogs are left to guess what do the human hand gestures mean. What do the , garbled sounds of human speech mean? How can we know? The human voice then is replaced by our own thoughts and guesses what it is that you humans are trying to say. The human voice becomes to us dogs, a bird cry, a groaning, a scream at which meaning we can only guess.

After a while even without knowing and thinking, we dogs begin to understand your language. Do you understand ours?

Let me explain, there are the sounds of the human voice your words and message which is devoid of true meaning to us dogs. There is the rise in sound level of your speech, the faster clicking of your tongue against the roof of your mouth, your eyes attempting to key to our souls, this all implies meaning.

Speak low, speak love, you smile, we dogs carefully watch.

There is the silent emotional language of feelings, subtle signs, hand movements, shouts, whistles, we watch your eyes for meaning. There is the sound of laughter where you humans bare your teeth in a free and friendly manner. We see each of your teeth, your gums, we intently watch.

Our hearing is very acute, you utter some words, and we are left to wonder what the meaning is? How can we act on that? Iucks a chance, sharp acuity on the dogs part is paramount.

I under stood Mary and she understood me, for looks are utterances, mute and expressive, a forcefulness of expression and animation.

At night while my dearest Mary slept, I watched and listened for any intruders, strange noises, the smell of smoke, ready at a moment's notice to bark and alert her to an emergency. She didn't ask me or have me trained as a guard dog.

I simply did this, because it is a major part of any great love to protect and look after those we love. In our lives as couples, and Mary and I were a couple, this was as normal for me as breathing.

Plus, with a wink and a nod, I had around two million years of canine DNA in our relationship, that went from me to infinity in all directions.

Gradually the rocking of the car the hum of the road, and let's face it, I was exhausted. I fell into a restless and uneasy sleep once again.

During one of these little dreams my feet started running. I dreamed I was running after a coyote in the sheep cot. Just as I flung myself at the coyote, I woke myself up yelping.

As my dear grannie Annie use to say, "Courage grows strong at a wound." She was, maybe on a good day, twelve inches tall.

Anne grew up on the family croft near Dunvegan on The Isle of Skye where her reputation as a ratter and badger dog was known in the whole of Scotland. Her nose was always twitching, and she found mystery and wonderment everywhere in the world around her, I am the same.

As I was drifting and dreaming, I felt the car slow and pull off onto a side road then finally coming to a stop on a small gravel road bounded by lamenting waterlogged bushes.

As the blond got out and pulled open my door a wet fridged blast of arctic air greeted my sleepy eyes and overwhelmed my senses.

Now I have a fine rich and thick coat of blinding white hair however for all of my life It was for insulation against the sweltering heat of the desert. I was not prepared for this first icy blast, it made my eyes water.

It was raining heavily; the rain was part snow. I had never seen snow falling from the sky. The ground was cold with a thin layer of white. There were people and dog footprints everywhere. Also brown piles of feces silhouetted against the white dirty snow and larger piles of feces with wads of tissues on them. Who can walk in a place like that, a mine field.

She pulled me by my leash over to a little patch where there was grass, and the snow covered in hundreds of yellow spots and dog turds.

As she stood there, standing over me, she told me to "do your business". I looked up at her inquisitively, I didn't know what she meant. Her voice sounded urgent and sort of rude.

Have you ever had to pee while some

stood over you telling you to hurry up?

Not easy. When we dogs pee, we need to size up the situation, who peed here-there, last and so on.

Dear Mary always said to me "Do it Josh" and I did. I did it on the clean sweet herbal smelling grass of Palm Desert where I was allowed to take take my time.

But how to do it here alongside a free-way where it was heavily raining sideways, where trucks, cars, buses, motorcycles, were all roaring by, mere few feet away.

There was not only that, but this place was so rich in marking by thousands of dogs, a sated thoroughness where nearly every inch of ground was a history of mon-umental proportions written by generations of squirming anxious dogs full as eggs.

This was the Rosetta Stone for me. Here were the exudations of the best and bright-est and the worst and the dullest dogs in the world. It is not just a matter of taking a pee as I earlier explained, you see we dogs of all types, mark our territory.

Standing there in the down pouring rain peeing, I again thought of, what else, my former warm beautiful life, now far south in the warmth of the Coachella valley.

My precious Mary cared for me as I supported her, we leaned into each other in almost everything we did. She was calm and kind with me and so I was naturally sweet and gentle with her.

Whenever she did almost anything, even the hot tub, she wanted, and I wanted to be by her side. When we sat together on our lime green sofa in the grand expanse of our living room watching John Wayne movies, we leaned against each other.

When we were in the cream-colored Mercedes, with our sweet maid, Angela driving, I sat on Mary's lap with my head out the window. I knew what button to push to make the window go down and up.

Every now and again she reached into the pocket of her white cashmere sweater and pulled out some Bon Bon. While she held it like a piece fine spun gold in the palm of her soft up turned hand, I would look at her sweetly, she would chuckle softly and say, "for you Josh". I would gently lift the morsel off of her palm pop it into my mouth and while chewing, watch the Bentleys and Rolls Royces whisper past.

You can see she was kind and so I was fed rotisserie chicken, quail and pieces of smoked fish for dinner. My favorite, though, was Greek lemon chicken hot off the grill from the deli section in Jensens grocery where we often went to shop.

Even now as I lay looking out over Puget Sound, I can see her standing in her spacious tile lined kitchen, with Frank Sinatra, Glen Miller, all music of the forties, on the radio.

I recall so clearly the desert sun slanting

in over Mt San Jacinto and across her frail delicate shoulders.

Standing in that ethereal sunlight she pulled little morsels of hot moist white, I like the white better than dark, pulling those little nuggets of white succulent bits of lemon chicken off the steaming carcasses and pop them into my white mustached mouth. When the juice ran down my cheeks, she was ever ready with a fragrant towel, to clean me up.

Thinking back, standing here, peeing beside this freeway heading to who knows where, I thought how iconic. Tears, salty tears mixed with oceans of fresh rain drops.

Driving further north the weather became much colder, and as a matter of course, much wetter. I was to learn that in the north it rained weeks at a time. Life, some lessons I just never wanted to learn. Is that called change, maybe so?

The blond opened her window from

time to time and when she did rain and very cold air swirled in around the inside of the laden car.

When she opened the window, I curled up and buried my nose under my fluffy tail. Sometimes though when it wasn't raining, I put my nose out the window.

You know, I am sure, we dogs' like to put our noses out the window of the car to smell the air.

What did I smell?

Well first the air was drenched, humid, thick as a slice of mold. It was not at all like the dry desert air of the Coachella valley. The Marsala cream on Mary's polished white fingernail, dare I say the neighbors' white angora cat. Everything was changed, accept it I thought, but in reality, I fought it.

Mary had been gone only seven days, it was way too soon for me to think of a world without her, even though I knew she was gone.

I am perishing from loneliness. You see Mary and I were a pair. Her love for George was transferred to me after he disappeared in a ceremony.

I know a lot about George, he was tall, think about this, he was 6'2", I am about maybe fourteen inches if I stand on my little cream-colored toes.

Somehow it didn't matter. 6'2", 14 inches" it was all about love and loss. You see George, I haven't mentioned him too much, was a tall red man, so I was told. When George disappeared, Mary bought me, listen to this, she bought me. We dogs are bought, sold, paid for i.e. slavery and misery for some dogs, but not for me. I saw a show at the Palm Springs Museum once where there were some pictures of a slave market in some place called the middle east. The human slaves stood naked, chained, while some potentate gave thumbs up or down, how ghastly.

Tonight, we continue to push further north to what? Rain continuous rain, in the desert it rains but not often, when it does it is still 90 degrees.

My name is Josh, my name is josh I keep telling myself, my name is josh: yet Mary, my Mary is gone, forever. Am I still Josh without her? What connects us to our loved ones? She knew me and I knew her, is this love? She fed me, petted me, kissed me, is this love? You see loving is often about seeing and being with the person you love, and, for my two bits, absence doesn't make the heart grow fonder.

With Mary gone well…

Without her its grief, chimeras, hideous jaws, a ghastly seething, a starvation.

Who are we, who do we become, when our loved ones whisper out of our lives. The glance, the eyes, the humor, the warmth, love kindness, yet somehow they whisper out of our lives and most importantly, out of our reach. Their voices disappear. How beautiful they were in their time. (A parenthetical thought here, record the voices of your loved ones. For when they leave, they take their dulcet voices with them). How I would love to hear once again, the sharp bark and rich tonal howls of my dearest father.

Reach back try to remember your loved ones faces, their voices, mannerisms, how they walked, stretch yourself, crane, no matter, the fog of remembering grows denser.

The intimate loving memory trail loses its ability for prescience, only our memory survives.

Those fragmented, fermenting scraps of remembering, those incredibly tessellated concordant and discordant glancing reflections of chopped, thoughts mixed with our day to day living, become like a ships churning wake. Remembering recedes, slowly dissolves, pales, dilutes, until tu-

multuous and agitated, memory marries
with the infinite until like the ships churning wake, it becomes a whole sea of forever
forgotten dissipated love and loss. Mary always held me in her lap, for me I thought I
would always have her love and lap, until I
didn't. This I call the sorrow of love.

Can it truly be true like I heard one elderly venerable elderly woman say at one
of Marys parties, "all love affairs are trage-
dies". I don't feel that way. I ascribe to the
obverse of that: "better to have loved and
lost, than to never have loved before".

So fast death, the angel of death, so
quick, so blindly blinding. Like a dog I saw
killed by a car in an instant, there and gone,
snap your neck, snap your paws, one in a
nano second. Gone, by the way, is a one-
way trip. No recalling, shouting out hey,
come back, gone is forever.

Now Mary is gone, last week was her
last party, seven days ago, only seven days,

though to eternity a blip, a feeble minor electrical event in space somewhere.

To be dead for a nano second or dead for eternity it is all the same.

Her last party last week was a party of her peers, friends and admirers.

Our fascinating home was designed by a famous architect, William F Cody. Mr Cody was one of the most prominent of the mid-century modern architects. Some weekends Mary guided tourists through our home.

Everyone said I was the perfect dog for our desert oasis. But then like I previously noted what doesn't go with white. Plus, I am calm, considerate, and despite some dogs reputations, I don't bite.

Our home was designed for shadow and light, like any great sculpture, sculpture is all about light and shadow. Large projecting eaves, that protected us from the molten desert sun, the occasional desert down pour of warm rain, and even more often the rain of truant golf balls.

At night our whole home, from out on the fairway, all lit up, looked like a Mississippi River boat at night, glowing and alive with reefs of candles. All our guests looked young and vibrant, even though they were Creme Brulé, from the insistent desert sun. Shadows and proper lighting soften hard corners, and age. As Mr. Cody, our architect once wrote, proper lighting makes your guests look younger. Tell me a society dame that wouldn't like that?

George, Marys dear former, jocularly said, "pink makes the wealthy look healthy". There were a lot of pink outfits at those parties.

As some wit noted, getting older isn't for sissys. This crowd in the desert, all felt "times winged chariots hurrying near." I can tell you now, I wasn't prepared and no matter what never could have been, her dying was a body blow.

Last week's party was another of her private parties, but weren't they all, she had that hard to define thing called, star power

At these parties Saul came, Hilda came, the famous old archaic beauty queen, Margo, still the toast of the Coachella valley, came. She and Mary, longtime friends, both had a passion for love and showy jewelry. The mayor came and his boyfriend Sunny, a tennis star, wearing really cool white and turquoise tennis shoes. His shoes smelled funny though, anyway they all came.

I had my nails done, Mary had her hair done, it was a full house.

And now, oh man what the hell, we are on the road still going north and me? I'm deep in thought as the outside world becomes grey in thought as well as in dreams, it's now me and the blonde, and Mary? Her narrative is only what we the living now give it. How quickly things change in this life, last week a party. A great party, magnums of Veuve Clicquot champagne, martinis in icy frosted martini glasses, wines of distinction, food of imagination.

Now? I don't know where we are going, increasingly the world is becoming black with a thousand gradated shades of green as we drive sliding under dark suffocating scudding clouds, it makes me constantly anxious. Change one doesn't see coming necessarily becomes playing catch up, not easy.

Take the blonde, I like her well enough, but she isn't Mary.

To quote a mouse, which I rarely do, "someone moved my cheese," and change is here, get used to it or die a thousand emotional and physical deaths.

Dinner was often served on long tables, al fresco, on white linen out on our lawn, under our towering palms. An east Indian violinist, this warm glowing night, sitting on an orange silk pillow played soft ragas, while a tabla drummer gently but insistently drove the beat. The talk was excited, the neighbor's cat came over, the dog next door barked occasionally.

We had chamois colored candles in sets of threes in tall silver candelabras lining the tables, cigars and port, meo-mio mi wasn't that a party.

One week only one week, seven days, one hundred and sixty-hours, five hundred and seventy-six thousand seconds.

Now here I am deep in thought as the outside grey world colors my thoughts, as mud from the lowering muddy skies seeps, filling up my little cranium.

Driving north, always north, we slide splashing under slanting skies riding on grey gusty wind driven rains.

The windshield wipers constantly push the rain aside from the front window. The blond has grown more silent as we head deeper into impenetrable stands of tall dark trees. The trees hang heavily over the glistening clammy dank asphalt like black dead cats, head down, spooky to look at.

At times she talks to herself, at other times she sobs then gasps, the air in the car is heavy with her sad anguished breath, her despondent vapor swirls. It floats like despair, all around the inside of the humid car, her anxious sad breath, makes me want to roll down the windows even though it is wet and cold.

When I whine, she shouts at me, when I am partially asleep, I hear her mutter.

As we push north, here and there are cataracts of clear water cascading out over great boulders, down mountainous rocky faces. There is in the occasionally opened window, the fragrance of skunk cabbage, muddy wetness, maybe fish.

Yesterday later in the evening after slogging all day north alway north, she pulled off the two-lane road coming to a stop where she shut off the lights to Stygian darkness. So profoundly darkened I could see nothing. I could hear Mozart on the radio, I could hear the whining of the heater and defrosters. She pulled on the dome light then opened the car door on my side, Mozart stopped. There through the rain, close in front of me, was a gigantic dripping wet tree bigger by twice around, then the blonde's car. I walked up to the base, lifted my leg and left my liquid fingerprint. I didn't smell another dog, just moldy mushroomy wetness.

The blonde turned the head lights on and I looked up the trunk of the ancient tree, it disappeared high in a foggy threatening mist.

The blonde held her coat over her head to shelter herself from the driving rain as she squatted leaving her mark in the head lights.

She then came holding her coat over the two of us as the continuous rain drummed a discordant roaring on gigantic leaves in the nearby forest pasting everything flat.

I saw a huge grey bird fly in then out of the head lights. We Scots are superstitious, I saw the owl as a sign, an omen, something in the future, don't think me prescience, but I saw a messenger. Tell me you haven't had some presciencent thought from one time or another?

The blonde opened her car door and reaching in, turned the key shutting down the engine.

Next, she grabbed my wet furry face, put her face right up to mine and while looking deeply into my eyes said, in a de-spondent voice", I am done driving for this goddamn miserable day Josh. Jesus Christ I have never seen such a deluge, it is so hard to drive in this, its like jogging in Vaseline, the rain continued without pause.

She opened the rear door holding her small flashlight in her mouth and pulled a monogramed towel with Mary's initials on it and attempted to rub me dry.

I could joyously smell Mary's perfume. What is it about scents. Each scent seems to lock itself in our brains, especially dogs smell this you remember that, over and over.

The blonde cleaned a place in the back seat, grabbing one of our blankets from the desert that still smelled of Mary.

Reaching down she picked me up and climbed into the backseat lying down with a jacket for a pillow. She pulled me close in that damp car in that soggy wet forest, locked the doors and shut out the overhead light.

It became eerily quiet and non-reflective jet black. Even I couldn't see anything and if you perhaps know anything about West Highland terriers, our sense of night vision is acute. Remember we hunt badgers in tunnels, and they aren't lit.

I could hear the rain coming hard again, it came in waves, first quiet dripping, then pitter pater to slate grey roar, then as suddenly stoped, then peter patter, the slate grey roar, then stop.

Once when It came drumming the hardest on the car roof, the blonde started to cry. I was damp, unhappy and not warm.

When the blonde rolled, which was often, I woke up to utter pitch black.

Lying there, there was a musical sound from the patterns and tones as the rain drops impinged on the roof of our car. A bit like the bells on the toy trains at the children's zoo in the desert.

As the blond settled down, she stopped turning and fell back to sleep. Lying there I could hear a frog then many frogs.

I wept.

The blonde rolled and tossed all night. I slept from time to time.

It was still rain dark when she leaned up on one elbow turned on the dome light then opened my door.

I jumped out onto the forests wet ferny floor and walked under the car where it was dry. I stood there for a while smelling the early morning forest scents. It was stone quiet. Then I walked up to the giant tree, left my mark. The blonde slowly got out of the car her coat over her head and left her mark in the headlights. The headlights illuminated a tangled forest as far as I could see.

Large drops of plopping rain fell from the enormous old tree.

When I turned back to the car, I could see that the windows were foggy. I could see the hazy shape of the blonde in the dim dome light. She gave me a piece of sausage while she wolfed down a candy bar.

As we drove out into the early morning dark I could see slashing rain in the head-lights. We drove over a cattle guard turned right on to a larger road heading north up into the mountains a place the blonde yelled back to me was "Shasta."

It started to snow, first little isolated flakes, then more until the road started to turn white, the blonde said, "Oh dam it Josh, we don't have chains," whatever they are, I thought.

Then in the next few moments it turned back to lighter mist then light fog. Then miracle of miracles the sun stabbed through the gloom. The rain stopped, for the first time in days.

Driving further into the steepening mountains the shoulders of the road fell away to white and jade colored raging rivers far down the broken mountain face.

Rounding one of many many corners

we came upon a large truck partially block-
ing the road, the blond slammed on the
brakes throwing me off my bed and against
the back of the front seat and onto the floor
of the car, I growled.

Jumping up of the floor this is what I
saw:

Staggering around in front of the truck
was a man lit by orange reflective flashes.
His face was bleeding profusely his hands
were bleeding, his arms were bleeding,
his driver door, on the monstrous rig was
hanging open. The blond pulled around the
stumbling man and over in front of his truck,
slowing to a stop, while putting her emergency flashers on then she went running
back. I watched through the rear window
as she stood in front of him taking off her
jacket, the sun was shining on her blonde
hair. She gently, kindly, with the look of a
nurse, mopped his bleeding face with one
of Marys Gucci white silk jacket, which she

had been wearing. She then appeared to pick pieces of glass, which flashed reflecting the emergency flashers on the truck. She carefully picks these from his bleeding face. I clearly saw that the front window on the driver's side had a huge hole in it the size of my silver water bowl in the desert. The hole was directly in front of the trucks steering wheel.

She came running back to our car. She was pulsing orange from the electric-colored flashing orange emergency lights of the truck.

The flashers in the early morning dawn projected onto her terror-stricken frantic face. She opened the trunk of our car, she was orange, then not, then orange again, then not, continuously. She took out what looked like a crooked stick, her face and body was flashing orange, danger like some rare viper. Then she went walking with grave determination, like she was mad, back to the passenger side of the mountainous truck.

Stepping up on the running board she jerked open the door, real fast like, while jumping back on ground beside the truck at the same time. Next, I saw her take the stick as she began beating something again on the floor of the truck until that something fell out on to the wet pavement, a bloodied grey pile of feathers.

She then walked around the front of the truck to talk to the driver. She took out her pen and wrote something on the inside of a paper match book like Mary used to light the fireplace with.

They smiled sadly then she came back to the car, threw the blood tire iron into the trunk and got into our car. She said two words, "Grey Owl". I thought of the owl last night in the car's headlights in that rainy forest. A sign!

I knew it was a bird, feathers were everywhere drifting on the light mountain airs. I had seen this before when our neighbor's cat caught, then killed small yellow birds by our house, yellow, red bloodied feathers blew everywhere.

Mary used to try to hit the cat with her broom, I saw her throw a bottle of suntan lotion at the cat once, she missed. Then she used to sic me on the cat even though the cat and me were friends.

Mary fed the birds and had a little pristine all white-ivory colored bird bath with golden tiled goldfish in the bottom. Maria, our maid, cleaned it every morning, and put in fresh lemon water. We also had a small red bird feeder hanging from our lemon tree. Mary never swore except at the cat. "Sic him Josh, get that god damn cat".

As we drove by the gigantic truck, its engine running, smoke was shooting straight up into the cold wet mountain air the driver shielding himself from the weather was holding the blonde's white Gucci jacket against his bloodied face.

Hanging from under the crumpled jacket against his bloody cheek was his pendulous eyeball which was wildly dangly from an exposed stringy set of optic nerves. He stood dazedly looking around dejectedly by his truck in the constant down pour. The constant rain carried his blood down, dropping from his chin.

The blond opened the window on my side, yelled across to the trucker, "Don't worry I will tell them". She rolled up her window muttering, Jesus Josh, I never saw anything remotely like that, his eye was hanging from his eye socket on his cheek, looking around so normally yet so abnormal. Sometimes Josh bad things just happen". I could smell her breath, and I thought of Mary, I thought of the face of the dying, now dead owl. Life, the owl didn't want to hit the truck, the trucker didn't want the owl to hit him, trajectories.

"Be alert, upper-level alert", as my old grandpa Angus Peter Charles Stewart, use to say. He told me once looking into my young eyes from his aged eyes; "Luck's a chance, but trouble's sure, I'd face it as a wise man would, And train for ill and not for good".

Bad things do indeed happen, people and dogs run into things, fall off things, get hit by things.

I have lived a long enough life to know.

Our old neighbor, Saul, is a good example. Down in the desert he drove his white Chrysler sports car with its gold trim, through the plate glass window of his barber's barber shop killing his barber.

He was wearing his white leather Italian loafers, one got stuck in the gas pedal. The Chrysler accelerated shattering both the barber shop plate glass window and Saul. The barber nor Saul ever recovered.

Saul used to give me milk bones in the

fragrant floral warm morning sun. He kept them in his upper left-hand pocket. He broke the milk bone in half and gave me one half at a time. He liked to hold me in his lap as we both sat dozing in the sun by the red and yellow rose bushes by the pool.

He patted my silky white head telling me stories, lots of stories of his life in a place called Oklahoma, where he said he was in oil.

He said his great granddad lived in a place call Bowlegs, Oklahoma. He said his grand pappy started an oil company called Chickasaw. I have never forgotten the name, since it sounds so funny to my dog ears, Chickasaw, makes me chuckle even now.

He said he had a penthouse on the top floor of a skyscraper he owned. He said he and his married neighbor to the north of him had sex on a large revolving bed he had had made every Monday night, like clock-work, she was punctual and passionate. He said his bed rotated, whatever that means, so he could see the sun rise and the moon set, what a guy.

Oil did that, he said.

He also told me. It allowed him to buy and run one of the Midwest's largest top ten, men's, fine clothing stores. He told me another time, "see god in everything, but watch for danger as well, think a little bit".

By the way he once told me, don't tell Mary about my sleeping with my neighbor, he smiled then he said, "she was also very hungry and I was widowed", then he and winked at me, and laughed.

I could relate to his life in oil since Mary uses oil on my white hair to make it, her words, more- glossy.

Soon after Saul killed his barber, his son came, very serious looking. They sat out by the pool in the sun, and I could hear them talking loudly, I saw Saul cry, which he did easily.

They packed a very small suitcase, and that was that.

Saul and his son came over one last time, I figured they would. Saul sat with me on his lap, like old times, he even gave me a milk bone. His son stood.

The Saul that we knew the clown, the dancer, the romantic, the collector of Russian art, the philanthropist, disappeared. And our wonderful Jewish gentleman, dear Saul, dressed in his black suit, cream white scarf, with his silk yarmulke, we never saw him again.

Bad things do happen.

Rain hit the windows stopped then soon hit the windows again, the sun disappeared and darkness filled in our forested world, the blonde turned on the windshield wipers.

Somehow, because of the trucker, I ended up on the seat by the blonde with my head on her leg, her pale warm moist hand on my silky white head.

"His eye, Josh his eye hung on his cheek and it looked at me. Josh that crazy bloody eye looked at me, it scared me, Josh. I can't seem to drive that image out of my mind".

"Death is everywhere"

The sun was out the next day as we drove through a large city with rivers everywhere.

The blonde started to sing "Roll on Columbia Roll on". That's the Columbia Josh, she was excited. I rose up and looked as she rolled down my window, but all I saw was a river.

As we crossed over the river, the blonde looked back at me and said "Welcome Home Josh", this is Washington State.

I said to myself, "my home is far to the south, I am a desert dweller. I am most assuredly not home! Am I Josh? Where is my home?

You see when your loved one dies—I

know now, for certain that is what happened to Mary, she won't be returning—strange things occur, none stranger than the death of a loved one.

It is as though the living want to erase your loved one.

They remove all their clothes, they sell their home, their jewelry, they hide the body in a ceremony.

Bad things happen. Maybe someday I will understand but today, cramped, wet with the blonde driving me further yet further north into the fridged wilderness, understand? in a word, no.

That's Mount Rainier, the blonde yelled back while opening my window. I put out my nose to smell the air and got wet from the icy cold spray from passing cars and trucks, for my efforts.

I am not sure what she said, she was excited, however I saw nothing except more tall snowy trees.

The blonde yelled dammit I looked up from a deep sleep, saw it was snowing again. This is the Tacoma narrows bridge Josh, she yelled back to me, I didn't look, who cared? The air smelled salty.

As I went back to sleep the road noise changed from wet to crunchy then to smooth soft suffusing quiet. I looked up, it was snowing heavily, the blonde was following two other cars with hats of snow. Their tail lights were pale red blobs. The sky was dark the road was white. Snow covered branches hung over the road. While I slept warm and cozy in my nest, I dreamed of Mary's smile.

"Here it is "' the blonde startled me awake", shouting tiredly, enthusiastically. "Here was what?" I thought.

"This is your new home Josh." She opened my window and I looked out as we drove down off of the main snowy road to a long snow covered driveway descending through overhanging snow-covered trees.

It was all white. At the bottom the driveway hooked around to the right by a frozen pond coming to a stop in front of a yellow building surrounded by more mounds of snow. Snow covered large rocks, small, styled trees, manicured gardens outlined in snow. I remembered, looking at these trees, the Japanese garden in Palm Springs. Mary took me there often to admire the Bonsai, all things oriental were her joy. I could hear dogs faintly barking at the top of the driveway and now stopping in front of the yellow buildings the whole pack surrounded the car, loudly barking, joyously barking. As we had gotten nearer to these unknown persons home my intuitive part took over since whenever the blonde came so did the tall blue-eyed artist.

I liked the artist he came with his children. When they came the whole house changed. The artist, me of course, and all of his children shot baskets, when the basketball rolled out of bounds, I ran and got it, great fun. As you may remember I like to chase balls.

As I listened to the pack of barking dogs out in the snow, there was a good sign, they weren't jumping up and scratching on the side of the car. I thought, wild as they sound, they must have some training.

The blond got out, then opened my back door.

She reached her arm in around my belly and pulled me out of my warm blanket with Mary's perfumed fragrance.

Then with no ceremony, she hauled me out into the falling snow, slanting rain and set me on the snow wet ground in the middle of this inquisitive pushing respectfully advancing group of strange dogs of all sizes and colors.

What a rude awakening, I was still partly asleep.

The snow was disorienting I had never

seen snow falling from the sky before.

One dog, a tall chocolate Irish terrier, whose name I learned later was Aston-Martin, kept walking around me while he pushed a dirt encrusted, rotted fetid seal flipper in my face. He wagged his tail while he did this and sort of growled in a friendly way.It was raining, snowing; the snow was drifting sideways gently through the rain. Standing in the headlights the blonde and the artist talked. I was starting to freeze and getting wet standing there.

Looking for the nearest shelter I walked under the dripping car to not only gather myself, but also to get out of the incessant rain and slushy snow.

Think about it for a moment, you know how I lived, you know where I lived, it wasn't under a dripping freezing car.

However, under the car I was out of the rain and frigid snow.

This whole scene was on the absolute

edge of my known trajectory.

Then, just then, when I was trying to disappear, the two littlest dogs of this pack, Pogo, a small runty west highland terrier and Tippy another terrier, black and white, short hair long-tailed, both walked under the dripping car and walked quietly up to me.

Pogo sniffed my butt while I sniffed Tippy's butt, Tippy then smelled my butt, then Pogo peed on the inside of one of the tires. I went over and smelled Pogos warm pee. I got parallel to Pogos pee and lifted my right leg and peed on Pogos pee. Tippy smelled my pee. then peed on top of my pee. We looked at each other, smelled each other's nose and feeling quite satisfied with ourselves walked out from under the dripping, heated, popping car.

The blonde grabbed me the moment I walked out from under the car and thrust me into the warm strong arms of the artist.

It began to snow heavily once again.

"Here is Josh, he is yours now. I know it was one of mothers wishes that if anything ever happened to her, Josh was to be yours. She loved him without reserve and I know she loved you the same way as well, without reserve."My unspoken dream in a tessellated world just came true. The fragmented pieces came together, we can love more than one in this life should we desire so, he smelled so fresh, I had loved him all my life, here now and in the desert when he came to visit.

I also thought to myself, who am I? I know now I am Josh, a dog. I am not a little human. Life of leisure in the desert can twist ones thinking. I don't ever think I thought I was human, but well now and then? Perhaps.

I remember the artist smelling like many things. He smelled like the sea, smelled like wood smoke from his beach stone fireplace, smelled like violin wax, the forest, good food, he smelled happy, oh joy.

As we stood there it began to snow heavily.

After handing the artist my bed, then my suitcase, the blonde gave the artist a quick kiss on his cheek, rubbed the top of my head, saying "see you later Joshie". The artist then said to her, "you look tired, I just made a rich Latvian stew, would you care to come down to the house, maybe a glass of wine and a bit to eat, before you get back on the road? "No" she said, her exhausted face twisted, "I have a lot to do, thanks though".

Then, just before she got into her car, she kissed me on my silky head.

As she was shutting her car door, I thought I heard her sob. Then her car door shut, turning on her car's lights, which lit the falling snow, she slowly backed around by the pond driving out and up the long drive. We could see her lights among the snow and trees as she drove out on the other side of the pond, and up the drive.

We all stood frozen by the importance of the moment.

We could hear her tires crunching on the frozen snow and ice for a long time in the crystalline air.

We heard her stop way up by the main road, heard her tires spin in the snow as she accelerated on the the frozen roadway and then nothing.

Just nothing, nothing that is, except, the gentle feathery delicate sound and sweep of tumbling white crystalline flakes, nothing except each flake is different, a marvel.

We all stood there in the lite falling snow for a moment, the snow landing on all of us like white lace embroidery. Individual snowflakes were softly visible in the darkening dome of light.

Looking up into the dark sky, filled with flakes large as my round dog tag, they drifted this way and that like thin white silver dollar pancakes, floating serenely to the white earth.

Then the artist gave a click click sound with his tongue, all the dogs came running, gathering around him. He clicked again, laughing as he turned walking toward the trailhead and down to the beach and our cottage.

As I started down the trail following the artist and the dog pack, I could smell fireplace smoke first. Second, I could smell the Latvian stew that he told the blond he had been cooking on the Round Oak Chief, all day. I smelled the incredibly rich smells of the sea, the wind ruffled cedars, the firs, I could see the snapping of a red, white and blue flag, like they use to fly at the club house in the desert. I could hear waves rolling over and lapping quietly through the downy sweeping snow on the beach. Looking down at the cabin, I could see warm glowing candle lights.

Heading down the trail to the cabin, the artist shouted over his shoulder through the cedar scented snow, "Great night to put up our Christmas tree, don't you think?"

And so, we did.

It was a very merry Christmas.

To author and artist Douglas Granum, creation is a way of life.

His inspiration is derived from his travels around the world and an appreciation of the unusual — trekking the jungles of New Guinea, enjoying plein aire painting in northern Urals of Russia, drifting down China's Yangtze River, looking at the stars in a Serengeti night sky, and commercial fishing in the storm-tossed Gulf of Alaska.

As an artist Douglas Granum works with and in various mediums including stone, metal, glass, wood, canvas, bronze and of course, writing. From creation in his studio in Southworth, Washington, his paintings, glass pieces, metal and stone sculptures can be found worldwide.

Find out more at DouglasGranum.com

Other stories by Douglas Granum:

JUDITH'S GAP

THE GERMAN MUSIC TEACHER'S COTTAGE

ALONE ON THE YELLOW STONE

WAR NO PEACE

OFF A LIGHT

THE ROSE COVERED COTTAGE

PINK LACE

Find out more at DouglasGranum.com